The Bunny Rabbit on the Moon

By Justin Chafe

"Bunny Rabbit on the Moon"
Written and Illustrated by Justin Chafe

Acknowledgements:
Page 27: The photograph of the moon, issued with permission from and trademarked by Michael Myers

Bunny Rabbit on the Moon
First Edition
August 2007

Published by Baboosic Enterprises, LLC,
PO Box 6102,
Bloomington, Indiana 47407-6102

www.bunnyrabbitonthemoon.com

Questions or comments: info@bunnyrabbitonthemoon.com

Printed in China

ISBN 0-9787660-0-8

Library of Congress Control Number: 2006907349

For Andrew, Zachery and Nicholas

O nce upon a time, a looonnnng time ago there lived a bunny named Little Mookey.

Little Mookey was very curious and loved learning new things.

"Mom, I want to learn how to paint," said Little Mookey.

So he learned to paint. First he painted flowers and trees, then a picture of his brother...

...He even painted his mother!

Little Mookey painted everything he could see or imagine.

But…Little Mookey knew if he tried hard he could learn something else too!

"Mom, I want to learn how to play music," said Little Mookey.

So Little Mookey learned to play the piano, the saxophone and trombone.

He sang and played anything he could think up...

...He even played a song by blowing bubbles in a cup!

But…Little Mookey knew if he tried hard he could learn something else too!

"Mom, I want to learn to sculpt," said Little Mookey.

So Little Mookey learned to sculpt. First he sculpted an owl, then a bee, then a pig.

But, he really wanted to make something big!

So he sculpted a big dog.

Then he made an elephant sized frog.

And just when everyone thought he was done, he sculpted a giant orange sun.

"Mom, I want to go to the moon and make a sculpture," said Little Mookey.

"The moon? You are going to need a spaceship," said his Mom.

So Little Mookey built a spaceship.

He packed his paint brush, a trombone and all his sculpting tools.

"To the moon," he said, and put a helmet on his head.

With much fanfare his little rocket blasted into the air.

Up on the moon, Little Mookey worked hard until his sculpture was done.

Then he flew home and gathered all his friends.

As the sun set he said "My new sculpture will be up soon..."

"I call it the bunny rabbit on the moon!"

Little Mookey's friends were very impressed.

They all agreed the bunny rabbit on the moon sculpture was his best.

Little Mookey continued sculpting, playing music, painting and learning new things.

No matter what he did, he always made sure to have fun.

You can still see Little Mookey's bunny rabbit on the moon.

But remember, the sculpture was made a looonnnng time ago, and is just a shadow today.

So, whenever you see a full moon, be sure to look up and say:

"I see Little Mookey's bunny rabbit on the moon!"

The End